OAKIE DOKE
and the
Nut Mystery

BBC CHILDREN'S BOOKS

It was a lovely evening in Oakie Hollows and Oakie
Doke had been tidying up his house all day long.

"Well, well, well," he said to himself, walking out
on to his platform for a breath of fresh air. "I never
realised I had quite so much rubbish!"

Oakie Doke looked around his platform and started to polish his brass doorbell.

"Still, after this spring clean I'll have the place looking as right as rain," he said, cheerily. "With a bit of luck, I'll be finished soon."

Oakie went back into his house and came out with a scarf.

"I knew my winter scarf had to be somewhere . . . oops!" he said, as he tripped over a stool. The scarf fell out of his hands and dropped all the way down to the ground, where it landed on Albert Corncracker's head.

4

"Mmmph!" mumbled Albert, crossly.

"Sorry!" cried Oakie, and he jumped on to his chute and slid down to ground level.

"I was just doing a spot of spring cleaning, and I tripped up!" he explained.

"Spring cleaning?" said Albert, in surprise. "It's nut-gathering time, Oakie! Winter's nearly here. You shouldn't be spring cleaning."

Oakie Doke took the scarf back from Albert.
"That's as may be, Albert," he said, grinning,
"but just think! When spring's here, I won't have
any cleaning to do!"
Just then, Rufus arrived.

"Hello, Rufus," said Oakie. "What have you got in that sack?"

"I've been gathering nuts, Oakie," Rufus explained. "I've got to collect a good store for the winter."

"Ah ha!" exclaimed Albert. "Now there's a squirrel with some sense."

Albert started to walk off, shaking his head and muttering.

"Bye, Albert!" called Oakie and Rufus.

"Honestly!" grumbled Albert to himself. "Spring cleaning at this time of year! The whole world's gone mad!"

Albert carried on until he came to Mole Bottom, where Manny Mole was busy too.

"What on earth is that thing?" asked Albert.

"It's just a little invention I knocked up. It's a water detector," said Manny. "You see, winter's drawing on, and last year all the ponds near Mrs Tickle's allotment froze over. She lost a lot of her vegetables because she couldn't look after them properly, so I thought I'd build something to help her find an underground stream or something like that."

Just then, Milly Mole called over to Manny.
"Tea's ready!" she cried.
"Thank you," said Manny. "I'm just coming.
Bye, Albert."
Albert shook his head and sighed.
"Tut, tut. A water detector," he said, as he walked
off. "I don't know. The only thing that needs
detecting round here is that mole's brain!"

Rufus was working very hard, pulling his sack of nuts up to Oakie Haven.

"Look, Hazel," said Rain, softly. Hazel was asleep, as usual, in her arms. "Your daddy's gathered up lots of nuts to feed us in the winter when the food is scarce. Isn't he clever?"

Rufus puffed and panted as he finally heaved the sack up and started putting the nuts into his special nut store.

"Hard work, eh, Rufus?" called Dave Squirrel, who was outside his house.

"Yes," said Rain, frowning. "You should be doing some yourself!"

"Oh, there's at least three weeks left until the bad weather sets in," said Dave, shrugging his shoulders.

"Three weeks isn't much time to gather up this many nuts," said Rufus.

Dave Squirrel came up to see how many nuts
Rufus had collected.

"Well, you have been working hard!" he exclaimed.
Dave picked up a nut and looked at it thoughtfully.

"Three weeks before the bad weather! Well, I'm
sure something will come along," he said, quietly.

That night, when everyone else was asleep, Dave and Denzil Squirrel came back to Rufus and Rain's house. Dave stealthily took Rufus and Rain's winter nuts out of the store and passed them down to Denzil.

14

Denzil took the nuts and hid them inside the hollow part of the tree.

"That's our winter store all sorted out then," laughed Dave.

"And we haven't had to look very hard at all!" sniggered Denzil.

The two squirrels ran away as quietly as they could, leaving the stolen nuts in their hiding-place.

The next morning, Rufus and Rain were horrified to find that their store of nuts had disappeared. Dave and Denzil were watching them from across the way.

"They've . . . they've . . ." stuttered Rain.

"They've gone!" exclaimed Rufus, worriedly. "We must go and see if Oakie can help us," he said, and off they went.

Oakie Doke was very willing to help.

"Tell me what has happened," he said.

"The store of nuts that Rufus was filling got un-filled last night!" said Rain. "They've just disappeared."

"Disappeared?" said Oakie, shocked. "Well, we'd better organise a nut search!"

Oakie Doke and the two squirrels searched every-where for the missing nuts. Eventually, they came to Mole Bottom, where Manny Mole was fiddling with his water detector.

"A water detector?" said Oakie.

"Yes. You see, this bottle of water acts as a magnet and the bell rings whenever it's near water," explained Manny.

"Well, I never!" said Oakie. "Just a minute – do you think it would work on nuts?"

"Nuts?" said Manny.

"Rufus's nut store disappeared last night and we can't find it," said Oakie.

"Well, I suppose if we were to hang a nut here instead of the bottle of water," said Manny, "it might be worth a try."

Rufus handed him a nut.

"I've got a few left," he said.

"Right," said Manny Mole, attaching the nut to the detector. "Here goes."

The machine shot forward towards Rufus. "Ooh!" he cried, realising that he was holding a nut.

Rufus dived out of the way as Manny was pulled along behind the nut detector. It carried on chasing him until he threw the nut on the ground. Then it stopped and the bell rang out.

"It actually works," said Oakie.

"Of course it does!" said Manny.

"Can we go and look for the store of nuts now, please?" begged Rufus.

"We better had," said Manny. "Off we go!"

And they set off, following the nut detector.

Soon they came to Rose Corncracker's house at Oakie Roots. Rose was very worried.

"Root has disappeared!" she said, in a panic.

"There's no need to worry," said Oakie. "We'll find him, won't we, Manny?"

Manny Mole looked unsure.

"If your detector works on nuts and water, it'll work for Root, won't it?" said Oakie.

"Erm . . ." said Manny, uncertainly.

"First of all, we'll need Root's favourite toy," said Oakie.

Rose ran and found Root's toy mouse, and Manny attached it to the machine.

"Are you sure this is going to work?" asked Rose.
"I can't think of a reason why not," replied Oakie.
"Right then," said Manny. "Off we go!"
"Good luck, Oakie," said Rose, and the search
party set off.

After a little while, the detector bell started to twitch and tinkle.

"Hello," said Oakie. "Root must be around here somewhere."

They turned a corner, and there, surrounded by a stack of nuts, was Root.

"There you are, young Root!" cried Oakie. "Your mum's worried about you! You shouldn't have run off without telling her where you were."

"I'm sorry," said Root, "but I found these really tasty nuts . . . I won't do it again."

Rufus and Rain came up.
"Any luck?" they asked.
"Yes, we've found him,"
said Oakie. "And what's
more, he's found your
nut store!"

26

Rufus couldn't believe it.

"How did they get there?" he said.

"I wonder," said Rain, thoughtfully. "I saw Dave and Denzil Squirrel up very early this morning . . ."

"Hmm," said Oakie. "I think we should have a little chat with those two!"

Rain was right. Dave and Denzil admitted everything to Oakie Doke.

"We're really sorry," they said. "We, er, we didn't think you'd miss a few nuts, you see."

"Well, they did miss them," said Oakie. "And you'll have to put them all back and replace the ones that Root ate."

"And I ate ever such a lot!" said Root. "I must have eaten about eleventy hundred squillion and – and three!"

"Oh, dear," said Dave and Denzil.

29

"Come on, you two," said Rufus, generously. "I'll give you a hand."

"Rufus!" said Rain, with a smile.

"They didn't mean any harm," said Rufus. "They were just being a bit lazy, that's all. And when we've got them all back, I'll help you fill up your own store."

"Thanks very much!" said Dave and Denzil.

"It's just like I always say," said Oakie, thinking of a very silly rhyme.

"Keep your head in the air and your feet on the ground,

For those who are lazy will always be found . . .
OUT!"

"Oh, Oakie!" laughed everyone.

Also published by BBC Children's Books:

Oakie Doke and the Lonely Mouse

Published by BBC Children's Books
a division of BBC Worldwide Limited
Woodlands, 80 Wood Lane, London W12 0TT

First published 1995

ISBN 0 563 40408 6

Based on the Television series produced by Cosgrove Hall Films Limited

Typeset by BBC Children's Books
Colour separations by Dot Gradations, Chelmsford
Printed and bound in Great Britain by Cambus Litho, East Kilbride